Dad looked at the water butt.
The water butt was leaking.

1

Mum looked at the hose. The hose
was leaking.

"Oh bother!" said Mum.

Dad mended the water butt. He put a patch on it.

"What a tricky job!" he said.

The water butt burst. All the
water came out.

Dad got wet.

Mum mended the hose. She put a
patch on it.

"What a tricky job!" she said.

Mum put the hose on the tap. The top of the tap came off.

Mum got very wet.

Dad got a new water butt. He put it on the bricks.

He got the hose. He filled up
the water butt.

The water butt fell over.

The water poured out. Dad got
wet again.

Mum got a new hose. She joined
it to the old hose.

She wanted to water the roses.

Kipper wanted to help. He turned
the tap on.

Mum got wet again.
"Oh no!" said Mum.

The children got the paddling
pool. They put it on the grass.

Dad got the new hose. Biff
turned on the tap.

No water came out of the hose.
"Funny!" said Dad.

He looked down the hose.

Oh no! The children got wet.